This Little Tiger book belongs to:

_____

_____

_____

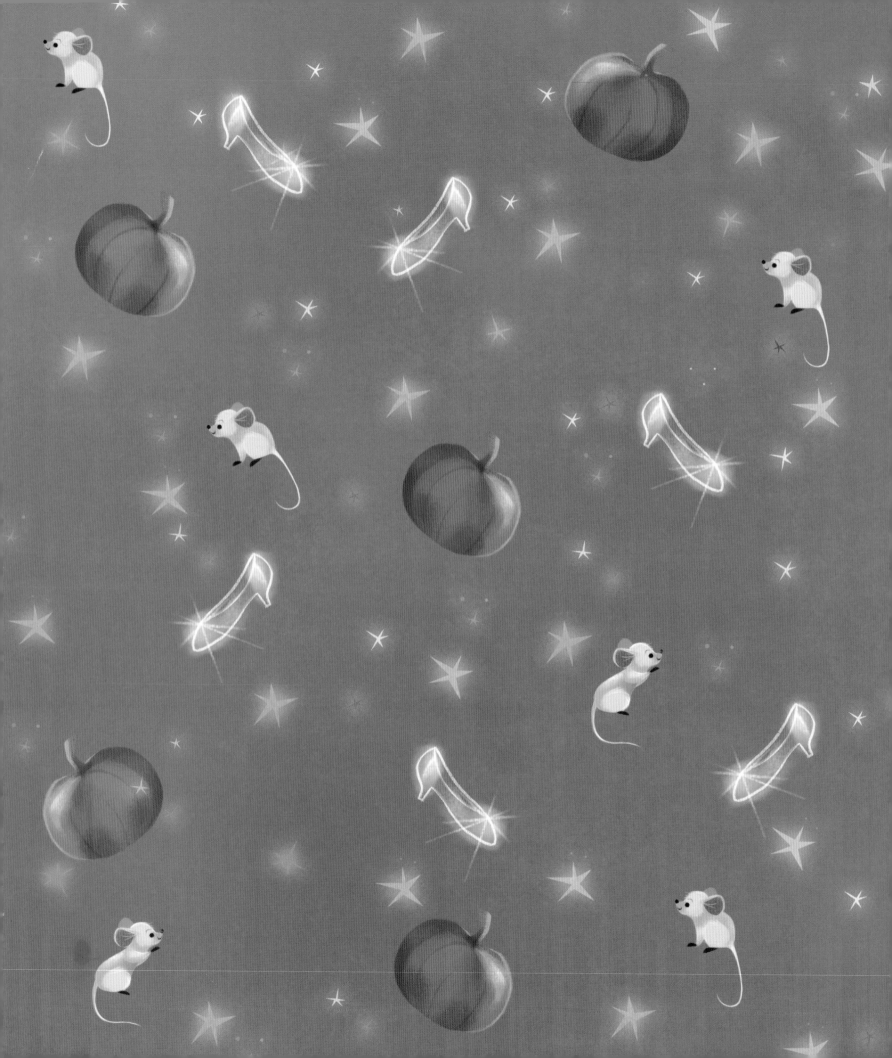

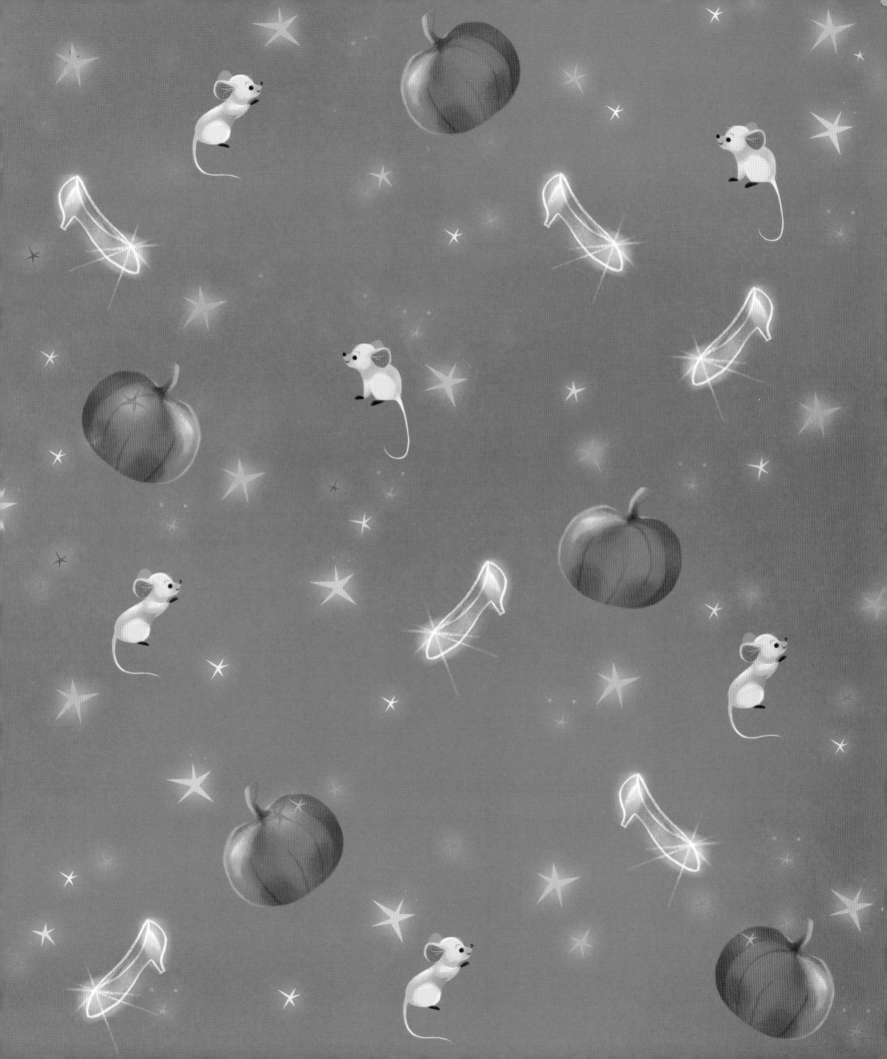

For my twirling, whirling goddaughter, Rosa ~ S S

To my favourite little Cinderellas, Chloe and Mia.
May you both always know that I love you very much ~ R R

LITTLE TIGER PRESS LTD,
an imprint of the Little Tiger Group
1 Coda Studios, 189 Munster Road, London SW6 6AW
www.littletiger.co.uk

First published in Great Britain 2018
This edition published 2019

ISBN 978-1-78881-337-2
LTP/1400/2904/0819
Printed in China
4 6 8 10 9 7 5 3

FAIRYTALE CLASSICS

Cinderella

Stephanie Stansbie

Roxanne Rainville

LITTLE TIGER

LONDON

Ella and her father lived on their own in a big house. Ella adored dancing with her dad, twirling and whirling until her feet left the ground! She was very happy.

Then one day her father came home with a new wife. She was incredibly beautiful, but her eyes were cold.

"This is Lady Davina," he said, "and these are her daughters, Minty and Jewel."

Ella was too stunned to speak.

Minty and Jewel cared about nothing but clothes. Soon they had bought so many, Ella's father had to travel abroad to earn more money.

"Look after my precious Ella for me," he said.

But Davina did not. She made Ella a servant and left her in rags. At night, Ella slumped by the fire with only the mice for company.

In the morning, her face was smeared with cinders.

"Here comes Smudges!" Jewel jeered.

"Sooty Snot-nose!" Minty sneered.

But if Jewel was cruel and Minty was flinty, there was nobody meaner than Lady Davina.

"From now on, we'll call you Cinderella," she snapped.

"*Call me what you like,*" thought Cinderella. "*You won't change who I am.*"

Don't worry, Cinders!

One day an invitation
arrived from the palace:

Royal Invitation

Everybody ~ that means everybody ~
is invited to the

Prince's Ball

Dress your best and put
on your dancing shoes!

Jewel and Minty were wild
with excitement and squealed
at Cinderella to help them into
their finest gowns.

"The prince better marry one of my daughters,"
Lady Davina hissed.

"I don't care about the prince," said Cinderella.
"I just want to dance."

Davina and her daughters screeched
with laughter.

"You can't go to the ball! The invitation said
'dress your best' not 'rock up in rags'!"

Ugly laughter rang in the air long after they were gone. Cinderella was left alone in the kitchen. Her tears traced bitter tracks through the soot and dust on her face.

"You don't want puffy eyes for the ball," came a
kindly voice.

Cinderella blinked at the strange lady before her.

"Do you like pumpkins?" the lady asked. "And mice?
How about lizards?"

"Er," stammered Cinderella. "I like them very much."

"Jolly good," said the lady, whisking her outside
and waving a wand.

Suddenly, there stood a gleaming
golden coach, with white horses
and a driver in a lizard-green coat.

Cinderella felt a tingle in her toes, a whizzy in her tummy and a buzzing in her head.

When she looked down, she was wearing an elegant gown – with sparkling glass slippers.

"Oh don't you look splendid!" said the lady.

"Now make sure you're home by midnight or you'll be stuck in a pumpkin with two rodents and a reptile!"

The ball was breathtaking. Cinderella danced with a charming young man. He made her laugh and sent her twirling and whirling.

This was *not* the plan!

When she heard the chimes of midnight, she kissed her new friend on the cheek and sprinted out of the palace.

The man ran after her, but all he found was a glass shoe, which had slipped off Cinderella's slender foot.

The following day, Davina was fuming. "You two are useless!" she screamed. "The prince didn't even look at you. He was too busy dancing with that ghastly girl!"

It's not our fault. *You* didn't spend enough on our dresses.

The next week, there was a knock
at the door and in walked the prince.
"I'm looking for the girl who fits
this slipper," he said.

Me! Me!

No! Me!

But the daughters could not squeeze their knobbly feet into the shoe.

Try harder!

Then the prince asked, "Is there anyone else?"

No!

"Only Cinderella, the maid," spat Lady Davina.

The prince frowned. "But I invited *every* person in the land," he said. "Take me to meet her."

Cinderella stepped into the gleaming glass slipper.
It fitted perfectly. And when the prince brushed
the hair from her face, he saw she was his love
from the week before.

"Will you marry me?" he whispered.

"Maybe," Cinderella said. "Once I know
you better."

We told you
not to worry!

"Fair enough," said the prince. "But what about these horrible women?"

"Leave them," said Cinderella. "They only value money, so they'll never be happy."

Cinderella was right. And when her father returned from his travels, he threw them out of the house.

From then on, Cinderella lived a blissful life. And she still loved to dance, twirling and whirling, with her wonderful family.

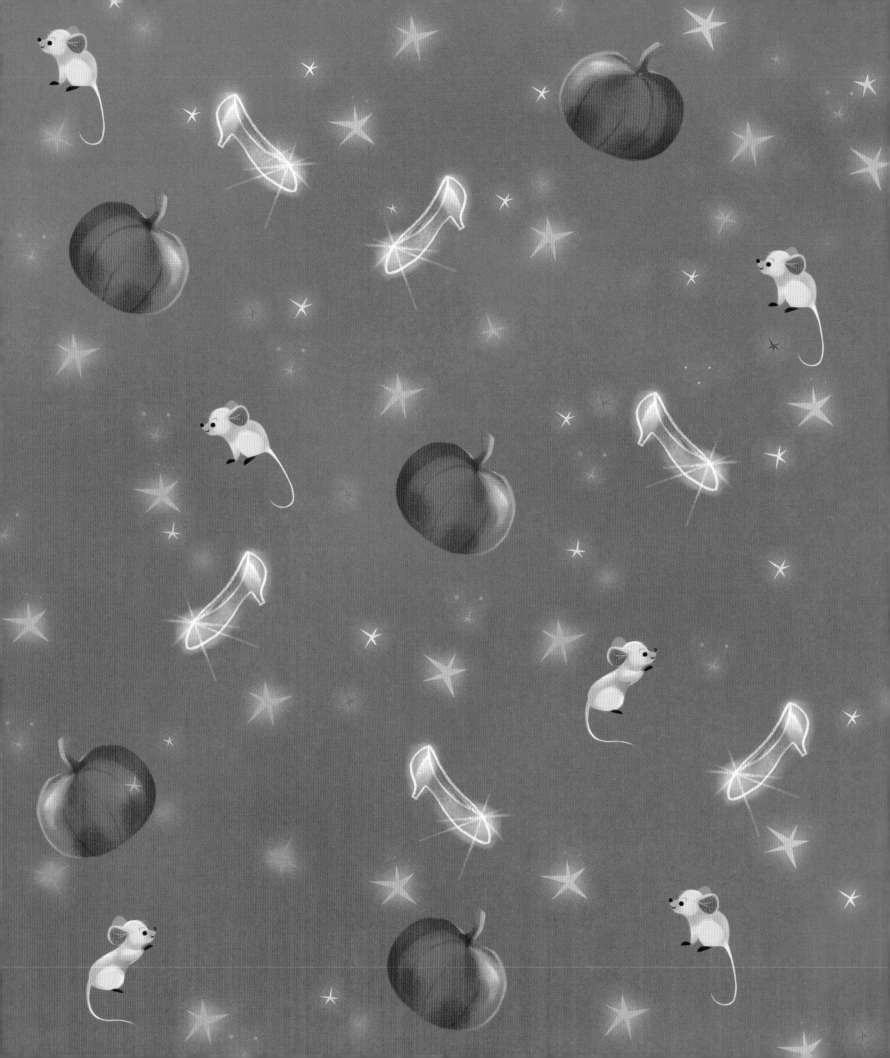

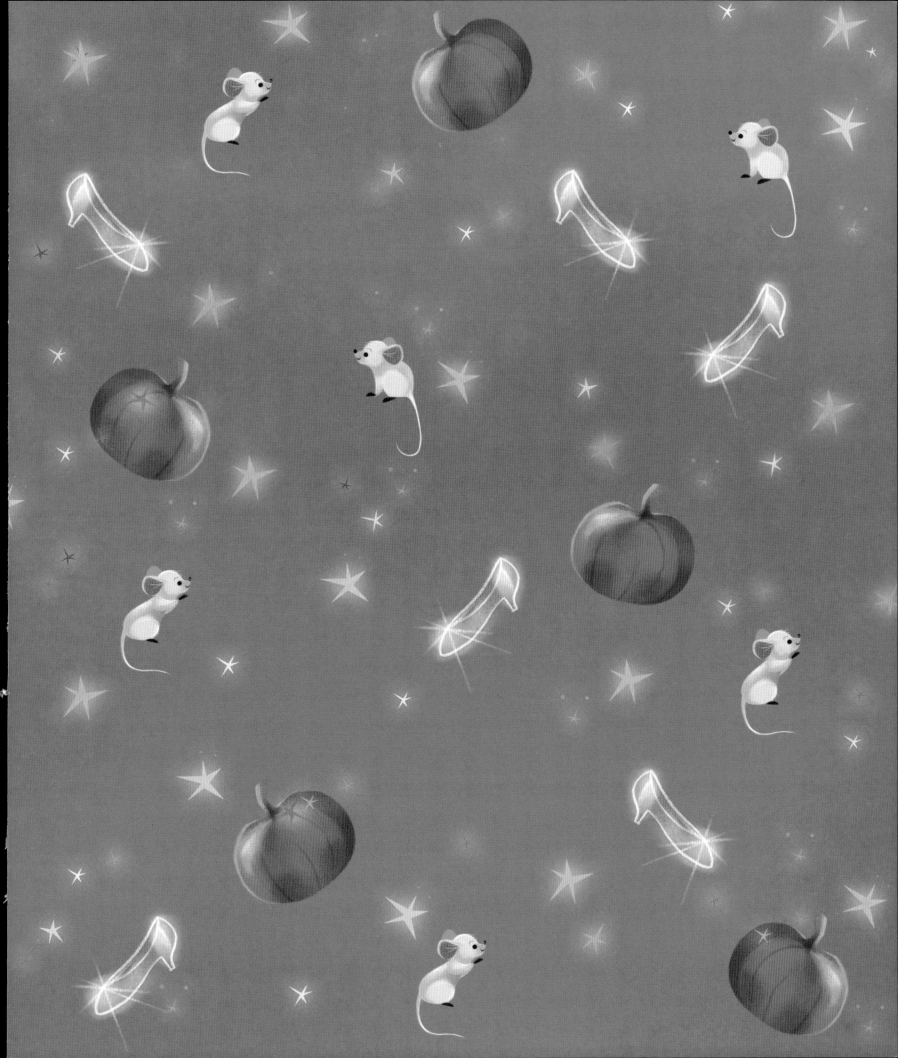